Dear Parent:

Congratulations! Your child is taking the first steps on an exciting journey. The destination? Independent reading!

STEP INTO READING® will help your child get there. The program offers books at five levels that accompany children from their first attempts at reading to reading success. Each step includes fun stories, fiction and nonfiction, and colorful art. There are also Step into Reading Sticker Books, Step into Reading Math Readers, and Step into Reading Phonics Readers— a complete literacy program with something to interest every child.

Learning to Read, Step by Step!

Ready to Read Preschool–Kindergarten
• **big type and easy words** • **rhyme and rhythm** • **picture clues**
For children who know the alphabet and are eager to begin reading.

Reading with Help Preschool–Grade 1
• **basic vocabulary** • **short sentences** • **simple stories**
For children who recognize familiar words and sound out new words with help.

Reading on Your Own Grades 1–3
• **engaging characters** • **easy-to-follow plots** • **popular topics**
For children who are ready to read on their own.

Reading Paragraphs Grades 2–3
• **challenging vocabulary** • **short paragraphs** • **exciting stories**
For newly independent readers who read simple sentences with confidence.

Ready for Chapters Grades 2–4
• **chapters** • **longer paragraphs** • **full-color art**
For children who want to take the plunge into chapter books but still like colorful pictures.

STEP INTO READING® is designed to give every child a successful reading experience. The grade levels are only guides. Children can progress through the steps at their own speed, developing confidence in their reading, no matter what their grade.

Remember, a lifetime love of reading starts with a single step!

To Sam, Cassie, and Luke
—S.A.

For Carrie
—T.B.

www.stepintoreading.com

Educators and librarians, for a variety of teaching tools, visit us at www.randomhouse.com/teachers

Library of Congress Cataloging-in-Publication Data
Albee, Sarah.
Elmo says achoo! / by Sarah Albee ; illustrated by Tom Brannon.
    p.   cm. — (Step into reading. A step 1 book)
SUMMARY: Elmo's repeated sneezes create havoc on Sesame Street.
ISBN 0-375-80311-4 (trade) — ISBN 0-375-90311-9 (lib. bdg.)
[1. Sneezing—Fiction.   2. Stories in rhyme.]
I. Brannon, Tom, ill.   II. Title.   III. Series: Step into reading. Step 1 book.
PZ8.3.A3295   Ej   2003   [E]—dc21   2002014528

Printed in the United States of America   14 13 12 11 10 9 8 7 6 5

STEP INTO READING, RANDOM HOUSE, and the Random House colophon are registered trademarks of Random House, Inc.

SESAME STREET

Elmo Says ACHOO!

by Sarah Albee

illustrated by Tom Brannon

Random House 🏠 New York

Elmo has a present!

What is it?

No one knows.

He is taking it
to Oscar.

It tickles Elmo's nose.

"Achoo!" Elmo sneezes.
Down blow
all the clothes!

Bert is stacking cans.
He stacks them
neat and tall.

"Achoo!" Elmo sneezes.
All the soup cans fall.

Elmo sees a person
in the barber's chair.

"Achoo!" Elmo sneezes.
Down falls all the hair!

"Look at what we built!"
the happy monsters call.

"Achoo!" Elmo sneezes.
Down falls the wall!

Here comes a parade!
The circus is in town.

"Achoo!" Elmo sneezes.

The clowns

all tumble down.

Elmo visits Oscar
to give the grouch
his gift.

"A stinkweed plant!"
says Oscar.
"The best
I ever sniffed!"

Oscar finds his hanky.

Then what does he do?

Oscar grins a grouchy grin.
And then he says…

"ACHOO!"

31